Happy Halloween, Sam!

We love you,
Uncle Peter, Aunt Liz, and
Summer :)

10-26-18

Library and Archives Canada
Cataloguing in Publication

Atkinson, Cale, author, illustrator
Sir Simon: Super Scarer / Cale Atkinson.

Issued in print and
electronic formats.

ISBN 978-1-101-91909-5 (hardcover).
ISBN 978-1-101-91910-1 (EPUB)

I. Title.

PS8601.T547S56 2018   JC813'.6

C2017-905572-0 C2017-905573-9

Library of Congress
Control Number:
2017951214

Published
simultaneously in the
United States of America
by Tundra Books of
Northern New York, an
imprint of Penguin
Random House Canada
Young Readers, a Penguin
Random House Company

Edited by Samantha Swenson
The artwork in this book was created with Ghost toots and Photoshop.
The text was set in Tox Typewriter.
Printed and bound in China

1 2 3 4 5   22 21 20 19 18

Penguin
Random House
TUNDRA BOOKS

www.penguinrandomhouse.ca

DEDICATED TO

PA

MA

Have you ever seen a Ghost?

OK, I don't want to freak you out or anything, but . . .

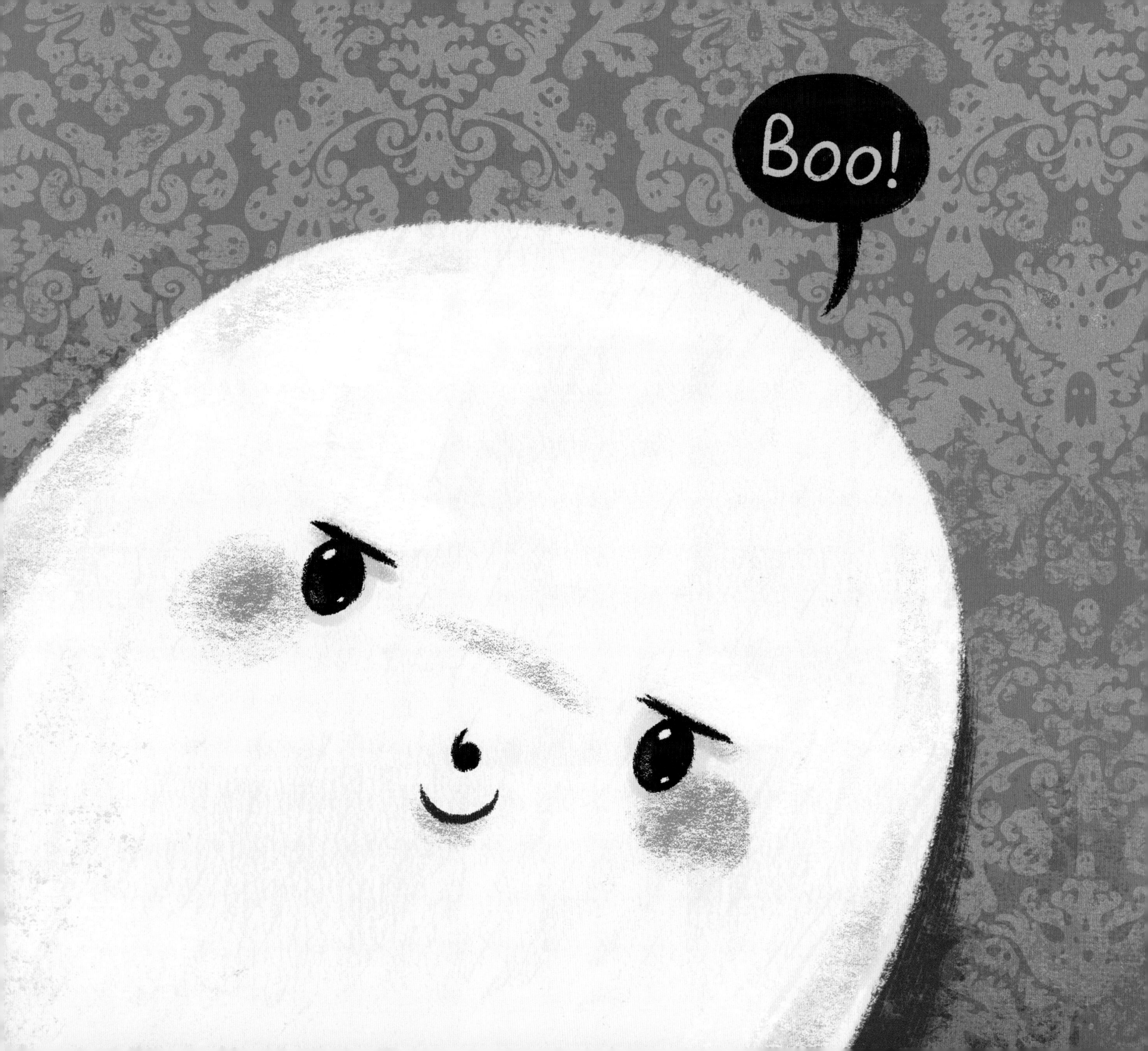
Boo!

It's OK to be scared. Scaring's what I do.
I'm a professional, you guys.

Check out my business card.

Sir Simon
Super Scarer
Ghostest with the mostest

I've haunted and
scared all sorts
of things.

I haunted a
forest once.

Do you know
how hard it
is to scare
a bear?

Boo.

Boo

IT'S HARD.

Things I bet you didn't even know COULD be haunted.

The good news is I'm being
transferred to a house.
My first haunted house!

The bad news is a haunted house
calls for more Ghost chores.
Oh, you don't know what Ghost chores are?
Well, let me tell you, they're the worst.

·237·

Have you
ever woken up
late at night to
stairs creaking?
Ever seen
a light flicker
or maybe heard
a door slam?

Well, those things aren't happening by themselves! Us Ghosts have a strict schedule for chores.

Once I finish my chores, I can get back to doing what I WANT to do.

You don't think I just float around saying BOO all the time, do you?
Borrrring!

I have a life outside of being
a Ghost, you know! Well, afterlife.

I'm into a bunch of things.

Cross-Stitch

BOO!

HOME SWEET HOME

PAINTING

Learning French

Anyway, here's the best part about this gig:
Rumor has it that grandparents are moving into my house!

THE PYRAMID OF HAUNTING

OLD PEOPLE
PRO: Sleep all the time
CON: None!

BABIES
PRO: Cute-ish
CON: Loud & fart a lot

TEENAGERS
PRO: Totally distracted
CON: Boring

ADULTS
PRO: Mostly too busy to see us
CON: Awake late at night

KIDS
PRO: None!
CON: Too curious

PRE-TEENS
PRO: Easy to scare
CON: Very nosy

In the pyramid of haunting, old people are tops.

Oh look, here they are!

Yes! That's one cookie-baking grandma
if I've ever seen one.

I've got to get a closer look.

The great thing about grandparents is
that they don't usually see us Ghosts.
We can totally slack off.

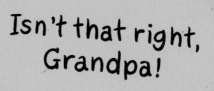

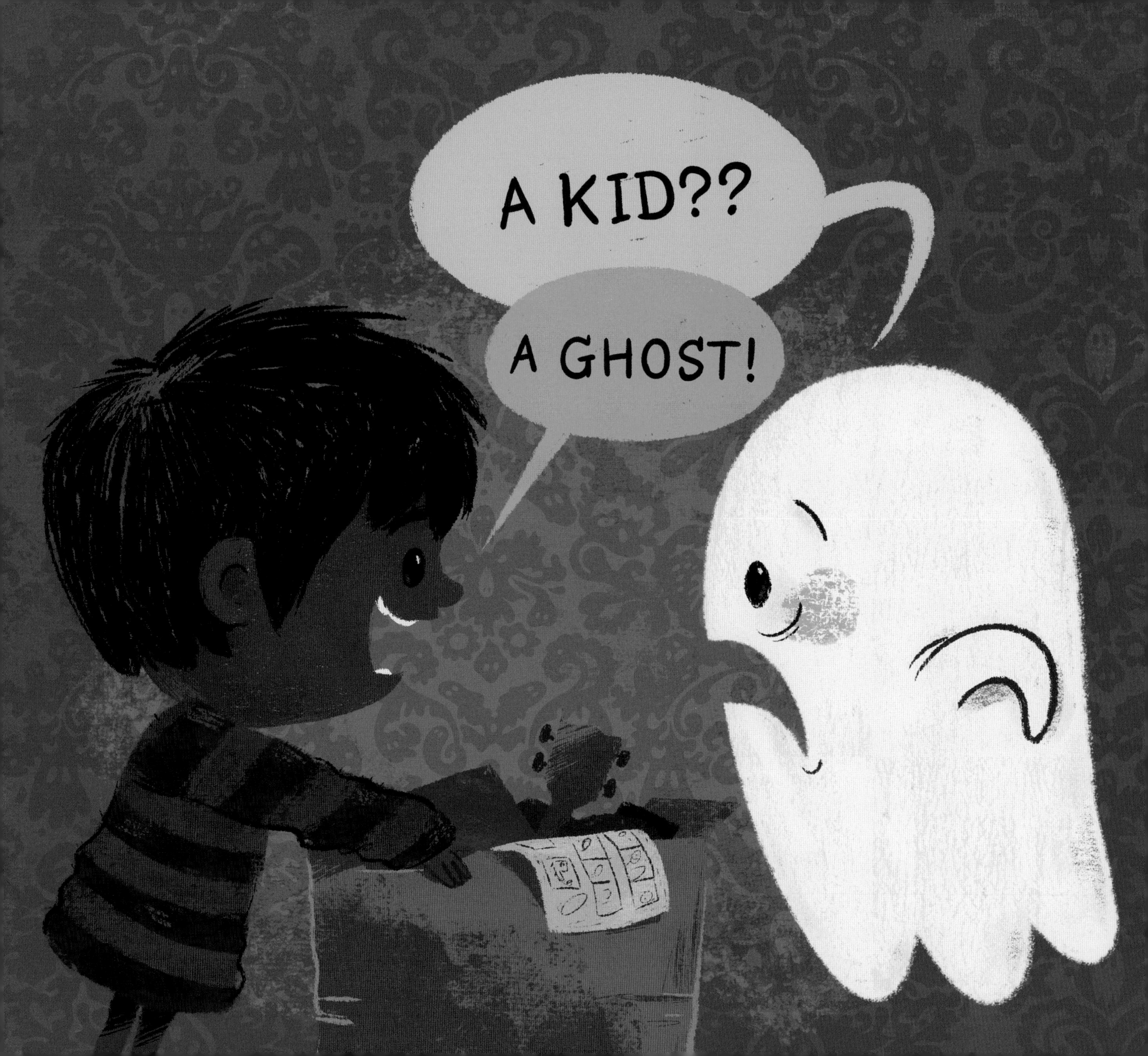
A KID??
A GHOST!

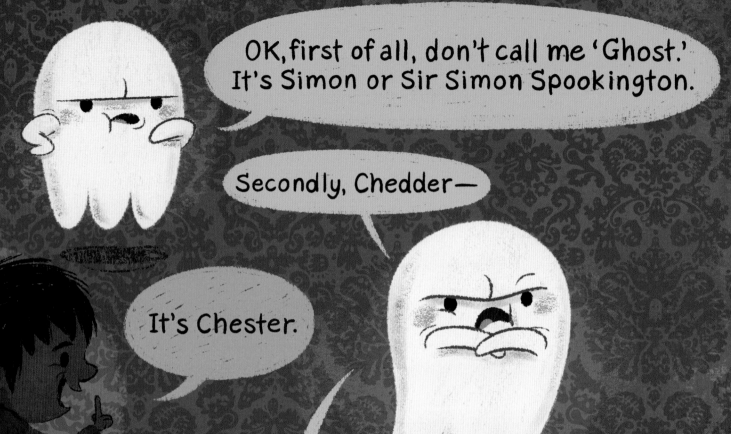

Chester. I think you would make a top-notch Ghost.
Really?!
Yep. I can tell these things. I have special Ghost senses. Come on, let's get you set up.

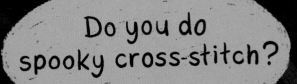

All right, Ghost Chester. Here's your fun activity schedule. Oh man, so much good stuff there. You're so lucky! Wish I could do all this.
Simon, you genius! All night to do what you want. And no Ghost chores!

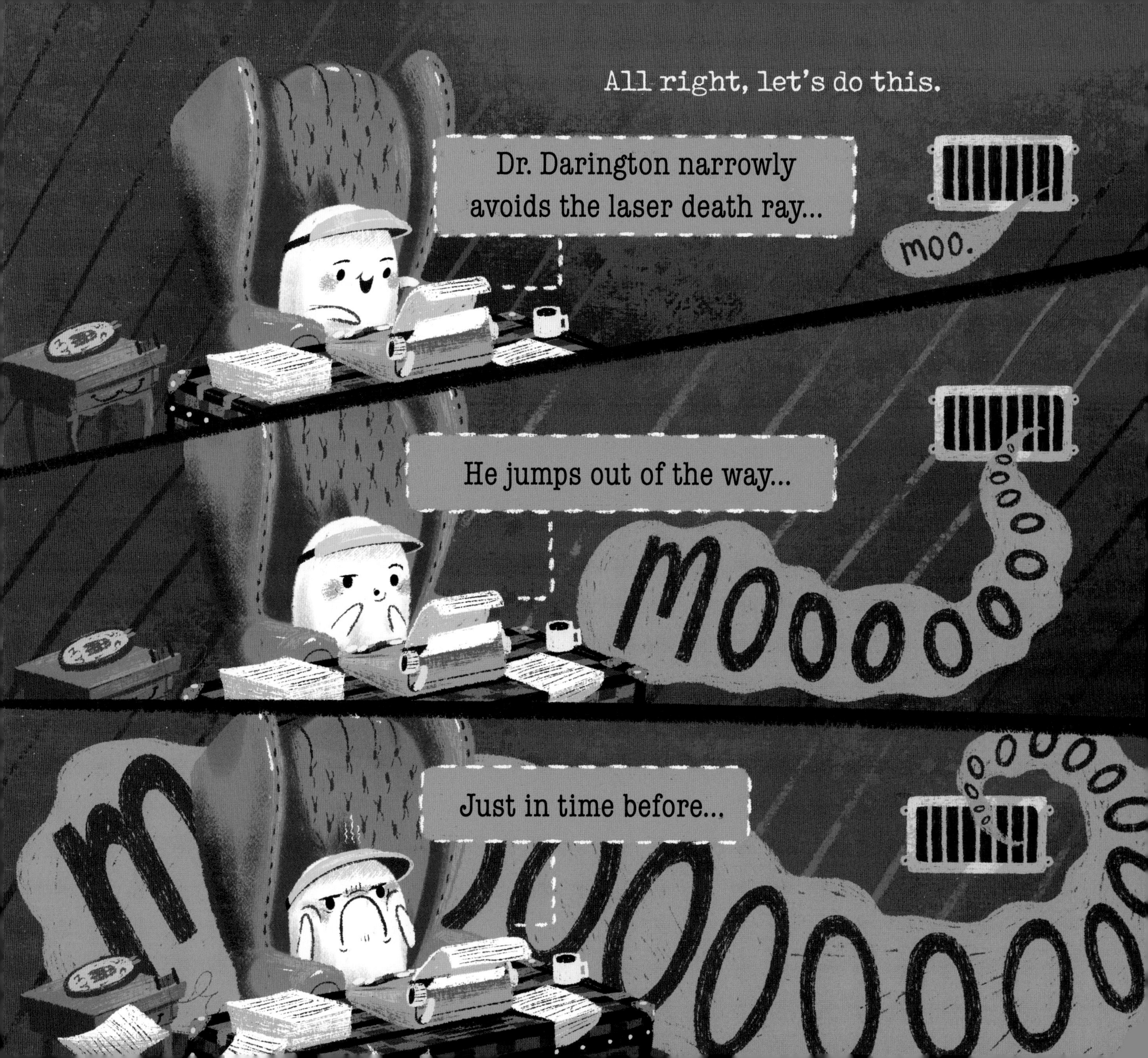

Well, I guess that's it for
Ghost Chester tonight.

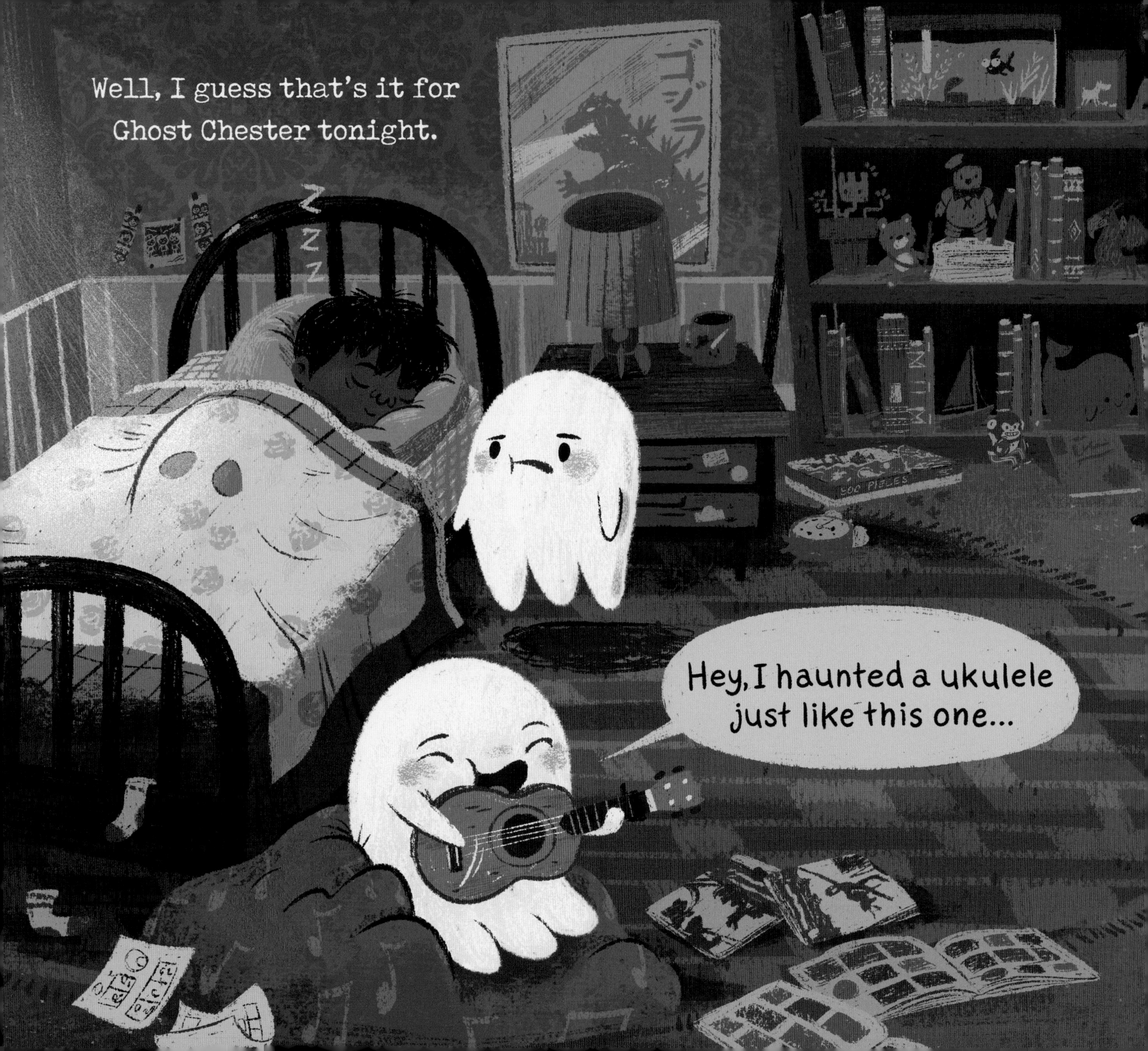

Oh cool, check out these rad comics he made!
Looks like Chester gets transferred a lot, just like me...

OK, I know what you're thinking. I should feel bad for tricking Chester into doing all my chores.
Well, I don't!

I mean, he wanted to be a Ghost!
If anything, I should be given a medal.

The award for most generous Ghost.
Simon the generous.

What?!
Stop looking at
me like that!

FINE!
I feel bad,
OKAY?

Chester isn't the best at being a Ghost, and I'm not so hot at being a human. But it turns out we're both pretty good at being friends.

DO NOT ENTER

AFTERLIFE

MONSTER MASH